Just Flash

by Michael Scotto

illustrated by The Ink Circle

WELCOME TO MIDLANDIA
OUR STORY BEGINS AT

Starring

Flash
A Most Unusual
Animal

No one in Midlandia really knew about Flash, not for sure. Nobody could figure out exactly what kind of animal he was. Not even Wilda, the zookeeper at Animal Land, was certain. Visitors would always ask her, "What do you call that big blue whatsit?" And Wilda could never answer.

"Well..." she would begin. "He's just Flash. No more, no less."

"He's strange!" the visitors always said.

Strange, weird, different; Flash heard all the ways Midlandians described him. He could not speak, but he could think and feel...and the Midlandians' words made him feel quite crummy.

Flash did not want to be strange, or weird, or even different. *I only want to fit in*, he thought. But there was a problem. There were no other animals like Flash!

One day. Flash got an idea: he would simply become a different animal. *But which animal am I to be?* he wondered. That was the question.

Flash watched a herd of gazelles at play. *They are having so much fun!* he thought. **Maybe I can be a gazelle.**

But life with the gazelles did not really behoove him. They were just too fast. They ran and hopped in circles, and played Ring Around the Flash.

After Flash left the gazelles, he saw a group of giraffes. *They seem so relaxed*, Flash thought. **Maybe I can be a giraffe.**

But he soon realized that he had picked the wrong spot. **They were just too mean.** They teased Flash about his short neck. To make matters worse, they flicked him on the nose with their tails and made Flash sneeze!

Flash felt ready to give up. But then he discovered a family of zebras. They were sipping from a brook near the tall grass. **Check out those cool haircuts!** Flash thought. *I'll be a zebra...that's the life for me.*

The zebras did not run in circles around Flash. The zebras did not tease him, either. They just ignored him altogether. Somehow, that made Flash feel even crummier than before.

I must have the wrong stripes, Flash finally decided. *That should be easy to fix.* Little did Flash know that changing one's stripes is always harder than expected.

First, Flash sneaked to the
aquarium to have the squids squirt
him with ink. But he and the squids
could not see eye to eye.

Then he tried to get some of the snakes to help...
until he remembered that he was **scared of snakes.**

The other animals were no help, so Flash finally decided to roll in the mud. Then he crushed up some white daisies and rolled in those, too.

True, he smelled a little funny, but he had changed his stripes! *I look zebra-tastic!* he thought.

When Flash came around again, though, the zebras scooted even farther away than before. *They must not like my haircut,* he thought.

Flash tried to style his hair with a honeycomb...but the bees told him to **buzz off.**

Flash dove into the zebras' brook to hide. *The coast is clear,* he thought. **But when he crawled out of the water...**

All of his hard work had washed away.
He was back to being weird, strange, different old Flash.

Then, Flash heard a visitor talking to Wilda. It was
Badge, the sheriff of Midlandia. She loved to spend what
little free time she had at Animal Land.

"What do you call that big blue whatsit?" Badge asked.

"Well..." Wilda began. "He's just Flash. No more, no less."

And no friends, Flash thought sadly. He wished
he could turn invisible.

"He's beautiful!"
Badge said.

Flash was quite startled. **Beautiful?**
he thought. *Surely she means someone else.*

Badge did not mean someone else. Soon, she was helping Wilda feed Flash his favorite meal of oats. "You are different from any animal I have ever seen," Badge told Flash. Flash bowed his head, and Badge could tell he was embarrassed.

"No, no...don't be ashamed! *Different* isn't a dirty word, you know," Badge said. "Everyone is a little bit different, whether you're a fish or a Flash or even a Midlandian. No matter what anyone else says, the things that make you different are the things that make you special." For the first time, Flash really did feel special.

That night, as Badge headed for the exit, Flash tried to sneak out behind her. "Oh, no, Flash," Wilda said. "Badge is a very busy Midlandian! She wouldn't have time to take care of you."

Please, Badge, please *take me with you!* Flash thought. "If Flash really wants to stay with me," Badge said, "I'd be happy to care for him." Flash lifted his head high and smiled.

Flash went to live with Badge. He helped her to keep Indiandia safe, and she fed him oats, petted his nose, and brushed his coat.

Flash never did learn what kind of animal he was, not for sure. Instead, he learned something much more important—it simply did not matter. *I'm just Flash*, he thought.

No more, no less.

Discussion Questions

Have you ever had a hard time fitting in with a group?
How did you handle it?

Name one thing about you that makes you unique or special.

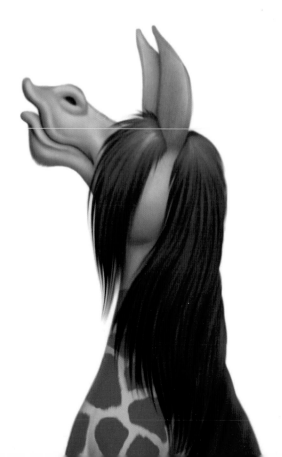